MW00789822

Saving Jake

Kaci Rose

Five Little Roses Publishing

Copyright

Copyright © 2024, by Kaci Rose, Five Little Roses Publishing. All Rights Reserved.

No part of this publication may be reproduced, distributed, or transmitted in any form or by any means, including photocopying, recording, or other electronic or mechanical methods, or by any information storage and

retrieval system without the prior written permission of the publisher, except in the case of very brief quotations embodied in critical reviews and certain other noncommercial uses permitted by copyright law.

Publisher's Note: This is a work of fiction. Names, characters, places, and incidents are a product of the author's imagination. Locales and public names are sometimes used for atmospheric purposes. Any resemblance to actual people, living or dead, or to businesses, companies, events, institutions, or locales is completely coincidental.

Book Cover By: Sarah Kil Creative

Editing By: Debbe @ On The Page, Author and PA Services

Contents

Get Free Books!

Do you like Military Men? Best friends brothers?
What about sweet, sexy, and addicting books?

If you join Kaci Rose's Newsletter you get these books free!
https://www.kacirose.com/free-books/
Now on to the story!

Chapter 1

Jake

It feels weird walking around Oakside without Atticus at my side. Since the day I got him, my therapy dog has pretty much been attached to me, and it's not far-fetched to say that he is my best friend. But walking around without him feels like I'm missing a limb.

When Dr. Tate approached me about dropping Atticus off for a patient to spend a little time with him, I was hesitant. Apparently, the patient hasn't been opening up to the doctor and thinks that she would be a good fit for a therapy dog but wanted to see first.

Normally Paisley would just bring in her therapy dog, Molly, who meets with everyone here. But after Paisley found out that she was pregnant, she has had some bad morning sickness. So, she's been staying home and in bed.

Working security here at Oakside has been the best job I could ask for. Not only do I get to see my friends every day, but I also get to feel like I'm actually making a difference in other people's lives. Besides Atticus, Paisley's husband, Easton has become one of my best friends, and he's also my boss, being the head of security.

"Only fifteen more minutes. I really appreciate you doing this so Paisley didn't feel obligated to come in," Easton says as he walks up beside me and catches me checking my watch.

"I'm happy to help. It just feels really weird not to have him here," I confess.

"Yeah, I know the feeling. Even when Allie is here is in the backyard with the other dogs, it still feels like something's missing because she's not right at my side," he says of his own therapy dog.

Right now, like always, she is at his side and stands between us. On a good day, Easton hates being touched by anyone other than Paisley. So Allie is great at forcing space between Easton and other people. However, she's more relaxed around me now. As if she could read my thought, she looked up at me and I swear she is smiling. I'd pet her, but she has her vest on, so I just return the smile.

I get why Dr. Tate didn't ask Easton to borrow his dog. Since he is head of security here, Easton needs her more than anyone else. Easton was a former prisoner of war, so knowing that his therapy dog has his back means everything. Atticus is to help me calm my anxiety and to pull me out of any PTSD episodes. Having him around and knowing I'm not alone has helped more than I could have imagined.

Glancing at my watch again, I see there is less than ten minutes until the end of the patient's appointment and I can finally collect Atticus.

"I'm going to head over to Dr. Tate's office. The appointment is almost over," I tell Easton, already moving off.

One thing I love about Oakside is all the natural light, so it never feels dark and gloomy. The way they planned the little courtyards was ingenious. Because of them, there is always natural light, even in the center of the place. An added benefit is that almost everywhere, you have easy access to an outside space.

When I get to Dr Tate's office, I check my watch again. Shrugging my shoulders, I figure it's close enough for the appointment to be over, so I knock on the door. I hear Dr. Tate chuckle on the other side before he opens it. Smiling, he steps aside and lets me in. "Well, you lasted longer than I thought you would," he greets me.

As soon as I stepped into the room, Atticus leaves the side of the patient and is right in front of me. Bending down, I pet him and give him a treat, letting him know that he acted correctly.

It's only then I glance up and see the patient looking back at me, her eyes wide.

"Jake?" she whispers. It's obvious that she's in as much shock at seeing me here as I am at seeing her.

"Kassi?" I say, knowing there's no possible way that my brother's ex is sitting in a chair staring at me right now.

Though she looks a lot like the Kassi I know and remember. So, it has to be her, all grown up since I saw her last. Her blonde hair is longer and falls against her shoulders in waves. She no longer looks like the young girl who dated my brother. Now she's a stunning woman staring back at me with full, kissable lips and bright hazel eyes. Her figure is beautifully filled-out with curves for days.

"You two know each other?" Dr. Tate asks.

"She dated my younger brother. The last time I saw her was right before I shipped off to boot camp." Even though I'm speaking to him, I'm not taking my eyes off the woman in front of me.

"We broke up a couple of weeks after that," she says, staring right back at me.

It's then that I realized that if she's here in that chair talking to Dr. Tate, she joined the military as well. More to the point, if she's here, she was badly injured. My heart starts racing, and this protective instinct I haven't felt in a really long time takes over.

"I didn't know you joined up."

"Yes, I'm a nurse in the Army. You went into the Navy, didn't you?" she asks curiously.

"Yes, and then I joined the Navy Seals and was medically discharged a few years ago. What are you doing here? Are you okay?"

This time, she glances at Dr. Tate before looking back at me, and it's obvious she's uncomfortable about discussing it.

"After I was deployed, the hospital I was stationed at was bombed. Unfortunately, I was injured," she says quietly. Though her tone clearly states that this is a topic that is not open for discussion.

"Well, I was going to go to the dining room and get some lunch. Would you like to join me?" I ask. One of the benefits of working here is any meals on my shift are covered. While the food they serve is all healthy stuff, it isn't half bad.

She hesitates before nodding. When she stands up, Dr. Tate hands her a set of crutches. That's when I noticed one of her legs was in a cast from her ankle past her knee. The blanket on her lap when I walked in had hidden it.

Remembering my time while I was healing at the hospital before Oakside was around, I know I hated having to explain my injuries. Even more so, I hated everyone trying to help me instead of letting me do things on my own.

So, while it pains me not to try to help her and do everything I can to make the walk to the dining room easier, I bite my tongue.

Leading the way with Atticus by my side, I glance at her a few times. I don't say a word, and she smiles when she catches me checking on her. Only once we hit the dining room do I offer help.

There are dining room assistants who help those who need it get their food, like Kassi, who is on crutches.

"I'll grab a tray. Just tell me what you want," I say, and she nods as I grab a tray in each hand.

After we get our food, she picks a table in the back so that she can stretch her leg out without it being in anyone's way.

"So, what is your story? Since you know a little about mine," Kassi says once we are seated.

"I was on a few missions I can't talk about. All dangerous. I saw things that would haunt even the devil himself. On my last mission, the building collapsed around us. Crushed my arm, and it didn't heal back the way they wanted it to, especially since it was my shooting arm. Add in a diagnosis of PTSD and anxiety, so they medically discharged me." I shrug like it's no big deal. Even though it totally turned my world upside down.

"So, is Atticus to help with your PTSD?" she asks.

"Mostly, yeah," I say, leaving out the parts only Paisley, Easton, and my doctors know about.

"What made you join? You never talked about the military," I ask curiously.

I specifically asked her that question because I spent a lot of time with my twin brothers, Brantley and Caden, and my youngest brother, North. During that time, Kassi dated Caden, and they spent a lot of time at the house with us and our mom. There were many family dinners and not one mention of the military from her.

"I hadn't thought much of it, but my parents split at the start of my senior year, and the divorce used up my college money. I didn't like the idea of starting my life in so much debt. Then I remembered what you had said about them paying for college, so I talked to a recruiter and ended up joining."

"How did your parents handle that?" I ask, knowing it wasn't good.

"Mom blamed Dad for it, saying if he hadn't cheated, they wouldn't have had to use my college money for a divorce, and I wouldn't have joined. All true. But I'd never tell her that because she has become insufferable to be around. I haven't even told them I'm here because I don't want them fighting while they're visiting."

"They weren't notified when you were hurt?" I'm shocked because the policy is to inform the family.

"I put it in my paperwork. They were to only be contacted if I died," she tells me, looking sad.

Ouch. This isn't just some small fight, then. She is really distancing herself from them. Just by how tense and stiff she is, it's evident that she doesn't want to talk about this much more.

"I get it. I didn't want my brothers visiting either. They all took leave to come see me. But thankfully, Mom made them do it in shifts, so they weren't all there at once. The upside is I wasn't really alone while I was in the hospital."

"You weren't transferred here?" she asks.

"This place wasn't available then. It opened after I was released and on my own. Though I wish it had been open because it would have been better than rehab at the hospital for sure."

We talk some more about my brother and my mom and other safe topics. Then we go on to catching up on people we went to school with and happenings around town. Because she was only a grade behind me after skipping a grade, we knew many of the same people.

Talking was always easy between us. But I still can't wrap my head around the fact that this is the same girl that would kick my ass in basketball every weekend and sat across from me at dinner, talking to my mom like she had been part of the family her whole life.

That girl never made my heart skip a beat when she smiled at me.

That girl never made me feel this nervous around her.

And I sure as shit didn't have the kind of feeling for her as I do for the women in front of me.

Why the hell are things so different now?

Chapter 2

Kassi

I'm still reeling from the fact that Jake is here at Oakside. Beyond that, what I'm feeling for him is very new. He was always my boyfriend's older brother and kind of like a brother to me.

After Caden and I broke up, I realized I missed his family more than him. I loved spending time with Jake, North, and Brantley just as much.

Caden, his brothers, his mom, and I would have dinner, then sit around and play board games and talk about what was going on at school, in life, or whatever the headlines were in the world. I miss that more than anything.

A knock on the door pulls my attention away from the past. I am thankful for whoever it is from stopping me from heading down the downward spiral of my life. Looking up, I check to see who it is.

"Got a minute to chat?" Lexi peeks her head in.

Lexi and her husband run Oakside, and they seem like nice people. Lexi's husband, Noah, was in the service when he was in an explosion overseas and was horribly injured. He had some pretty bad scarring. Unfortunately, back then, there was no place like Oakside for him.

This place was born from his need. I will say I'd much rather be here than in a hospital.

My room feels more like a bed-and-breakfast than a medical facility. I have my own bathroom, for which I'm grateful. The room is decorated to feel comfortable and rustic. I have a bed, a desk, and even a living space with a couch and a TV.

"I don't know. Let me check my super busy social calendar," I say, stopping the eye roll I wanted to include.

In reality, Lexi knows my calendar better than I do. She is super involved with all the patients here at Oakside and makes sure they are keeping up with treatments and have everything they need.

Ignoring my sarcastic comment, she smiles, joining me on the couch.

"Rumor has it that you know Jake?" she asks.

Good lord, Oakside's rumor mill works faster than most small towns. It's been less than an hour since I had lunch with Jake in the dining room.

"What rumor?" I ask.

"The one where he came and told me," she laughs.

My heart thunders in my chest. Why would he do that? It's not a big deal that we know each other. I like to think we were friends way back when I dated his brother, so it was nothing more than friends catching up, right?

"What did he say?" I ask, not wanting to give away more than he already did.

"That you dated his brother, and he wanted us to know. After talking to him, I wanted to come and make sure you are okay with him being around while you are here. He wanted to make sure as well. If you would rather not see or run into him, I can make that happen. He was adamant that he doesn't want to be the reason you aren't healing or feel like you can't open up to the staff here."

That is oddly sweet of him. But If I had a problem with him, I wouldn't have gone and had lunch with him. Then a thought hits me. What if this is his way of looking for an out because he doesn't want to run into me while here?

"I won't be the reason he loses his job." I shake my head, not knowing what else to say.

"Oh no, he's a good guy. I wouldn't do that. I'd just reassign him while you are here. We have plenty to do in the offices we need help with."

Somehow, I don't think he'd be overly happy working in an office all day. That never seemed like him.

"Well, I don't mind him being here. It was nice to see him and catch up."

"And here I thought you only talked to me." She acts offended, but there is a smile on her face.

She isn't wrong. Before Jake, I really didn't talk to anyone other than her. Lexi has a way of making you feel comfortable. We didn't talk about my accident or even my military time. She just wanted to get to know me, and she made it really easy to like her.

"So, how long have you known Jake?" she asks, getting comfortable on the couch.

"My family moved to town in middle school, and I became friends with his twin brothers Brentley and Caden. Then Caden and I started to date in our junior year. I spent a lot of time at his place, and that was when I got to know Jake as well. He was in a different grade, so until then, we didn't cross paths much. Same with their younger brother North."

"Did you and his brother end on good terms?"

"Yeah. We were going our separate ways. Wanted different things." I shrug, not really wanting to get into it.

"But you and Jake left it on good terms?" she asks hesitantly.

"By the time Caden and I broke up, he was in boot camp. This is the first time I've seen him since."

"Okay, well, if it's too much for him to be around you at any point, let me know, and I'll take care of it. Your recovery is the most important thing," she says, standing with a smile.

Or lack of recovery, I think, because I feel like I'm not making an ounce of progress.

The doctors keep telling me I won't see the progress because it's little changes day by day. But most days, I feel like I'm going backward, not forward. It's hard to see an end to it all, and it feels like my recovery will last forever.

Finally, to distract myself, I flip on the TV and binge-watch the small-town rom-com TV show I've been absorbed in. Getting lost in someone else's problems seems to be the best way of dealing with everything going on in my life right now.

Chapter 3

Jake

I'm making my morning rounds around Oakside when Dr. Tate steps out of his office.

"Jake, I'm glad to see you. Do you have a minute?" he asks.

"Sure, is everything okay?" I ask, following him back into his office.

The sun shines through the large windows, and Atticus lies down on the hardwood floor in the light cast by the sun onto the floor. For a moment, I'm jealous of him being able to soak up the warmth of the sun on this cool Georgia winter day.

"Lexi told me she talked to Kassi and that she is comfortable with you being around. So, I wanted to ask you a favor," he says, leaning against his desk.

"I'm happy to help if I can," I tell him, not sure where this is going.

"I've been meeting with Kassi for over a month now, and she barely talks in our sessions and usually nothing more than one-word answers and only when asked direct questions. That is until she saw you."

"Isn't that how most people act during therapy? I know I wasn't an easy patient. I didn't want to talk at first because I just wasn't ready to." Though even now, I try not to think of my time in therapy especially at the beginning. I wasn't a great patient.

Oakside may not have been around when I was in my healing process, but Dr. Tate was my therapist, and I was at the hospital. So, we have a history.

"Some people have trouble opening up. But I feel like there's another block in there with her. It's a feeling I have, and I've been doing this long enough to trust my gut," he says.

"Alright, but what does this have to do with me?"

"I'm hoping you're willing to spend a little time with her. Get her talking not necessarily about the accident but just in general. Have her talk about her time in the military leading up to this last deployment or anything, really. It might help her open up in therapy. Just by getting her talking to you, it can spill over to our sessions."

I hesitate. Part of me knows if she found out about this, she would be more than mad. The other part of me wants to help her out, no matter what. I know she has to talk to Dr. Tate. In order to truly heal and move on, she has to open up. What surprises me is that all of a sudden, I want that for her more than my next breath.

"Okay, after my shift today, I will give it a try," I tell him. The big, friendly smile he's known for crosses his face. "Thanks, Jake. What is said between you two is your business. There's no need to report back unless you feel like it's something that absolutely should be shared." Then he goes to his desk, leaving me alone with my thoughts.

As I make the rounds for my shift, I notice that even Atticus is checking in on me more. I guess Dr. Tate's request and the thought of spending time with Kassi has me a little on edge.

I meant what I said that, I would do anything to help her recovery. Something in my gut says that this is almost like spending time with her under false pretenses. I know she wouldn't open up to me if I told her, but I also feel like I'm in a tough spot because if she finds out that I'm there because I was asked to be, it might be just as bad or worse.

I'm on the back porch of the main building at Oakside, watching some guys doing yoga class on the back lawn, when Atticus nudges me to sit down in a nearby chair. That alone indicates he's worried about me. I give him a treat and then sit and pet him.

Just the simple act of petting him has always calmed me down. Today is no different. Sitting here with him helps me realize that no matter the outcome, the goal is to help Kassi get better. If she ends up mad at me but back up on her feet, so be it. That's a risk I'm willing to take.

The problem is, I don't know how to get her to open up. It's not like we have this big connection. It's been years since we've talked, and at lunch the other day, I did most of the talking.

Glancing at my watch, I realize I've only got about thirty minutes left of my shift, which ends at three o'clock. I should go talk to Lexi, find out what the schedule is for the day, and make a game plan.

Walking downstairs to the offices, I find Lexi at her desk and her husband Noah sitting on the couch at the side of her desk, book in hand. Since the door is wide open, I give a soft tap on the doorway to let them know that I'm there.

They both look up and smile at me. "Jake, come on in," Noah says, setting the book down.

I take a seat on the chair across from Lexi's desk, and Atticus sits beside me. Without thinking, like a reflex, I reach out and pet him.

"Dr. Tate asked me to spend some time with Kassi to see if I couldn't get her talking outside of his office. Apparently, she's not talking to anyone, and the most she talked to anyone was when we had lunch together the other day. Is that correct?"

Noah and Lexi share a look.

"Yeah, she barely talks to the nurses and gives one-word answers. When asked a direct question, it's like she's completely shut down," Noah says.

"You two have a history before the accident, and there's a good chance that you can use that and those connections to pull her out of her shell," Lexi says. "If you're not comfortable, don't even worry about it. I don't ever want to put you in a position to do something that you're not comfortable with."

"I'm happy to help. Though I wish I had known she was here sooner." Taking a deep breath, I look down at Atticus, who rests his head in my lap, looking up at me as I pet him.

"I'm off at three. Are you able to tell me what her schedule looks like today? I hate to pop in minutes before she's supposed to be off doing something else."

At my words, a smile crosses both their faces.

Lexi turns to her computer and starts tapping on the keyboard. A moment later, she turns back to me.

"She is free for the rest of the day. It looks like, in general, all of her appointments are in the morning, and she keeps her afternoons free."

"Perfect, I work mornings, and I'm usually off by two or three," I say as an idea starts to form in my head.

She'd spend a lot of time after school with my brothers and me at our house. We get out of school by three. My mom would have a snack for us, and we'd do our homework and play board games until dinner time. But no matter what, that time before dinner was always family time.

After dinner, she and Caden would have time to themselves. Maybe they'd go out on a date or spend some time in the backyard alone.

She was always competitive, but you have to be when you're playing a game against other boys. Even though we'd play card games, she always seemed to enjoy and smile more when we played the board games.

"You wouldn't by chance have any board games around here with you?" I ask.

"We have a bunch of them in the cabinets in the library," Noah says. "I'll show you where."

He stands, and I follow him back upstairs down the same hallway where a lot of the offices are.

The library here is huge. It is one of the original rooms that they kept from the house but expanded it. They did such a good job of matching the bookcases that were already there that you couldn't tell which ones were the original and which ones were the ones that were built for Oakside.

Noah opens a cabinet, and inside are stacks and stacks of board games. One catches my attention right away. Memories of her playing, her smiles, and just how carefree she was came to mind as I reach out and pick it up.

"This one's perfect." I stay with a grin, turning and heading to her room.

Chapter 4

Kassi

Right now, I'm snuggled up on my couch under a blanket, reading a mafia romance about a morally gray hero. I'm trying to get lost in a whole other world than the one I'm currently trapped in.

I've always been a bit of a hopeless romantic, wanting someone to love me to the point of obsession, picking me over everyone else.

The problem is guys around me lately are the self-absorbed enlisted military men who think they're God's gift to women.

I've been on a few dates since I joined, but my options are so limited. Either date a guy outside the military who doesn't get it and is intimidated by a stronger female than him or date one of the servicemen that I have to prove I actually belong in the military.

Needless to say, in my situation, it's easier to get lost in the arms of a book boyfriend than to date.

I've been able to schedule all my appointments each day in the morning, which leaves me the afternoon to go through my to-be-read list and actually get to read. Since I've begun, I've been reading about a book a day. Noah and Lexi have been amazing in getting me a tablet that I can use and binge-read on.

Today, I'm at the point in the book when the morally gray hero realizes she is his everything when there's a knock on the door. I actually groan out loud about having to set the book down, as no one usually interrupts me after lunch.

"If it's that painful to set your book down, then I can come back," Jake says from the doorway, raising an eyebrow at me.

"How did you know I was reading?" I ask, setting my tablet on the coffee table and waving him into the room.

"Because whenever you read, you snuggle up under a big thick blanket like you're doing now. You always have," he says.

Did he always know me this well? How did I miss that? That's when I notice he's holding one of his hands behind his back.

"What do you have that you're hiding?" I ask, nodding his way.

"Well, I saw this in the library, and it made me think of you. I was wondering if you wanted to play with me?" He pulls out a box from behind his back and steps forward, turning it so I can see what's on the cover.

"Payday?!" I'm unable to hide my excitement.

It's one of my favorite board games. We would play it when I was over at his house. Though I haven't played it since Caden and I broke up, and seeing it now reminds me of all the fun and carefree times we had. Instantly, with all my heart, all I want to do is play that game. My book and the hero are easily forgotten.

"Do you have time to play?" I ask since he's on the clock.

"My shift just ended, so if you'll have me, I'd love to play with you," he says with a smile. Then he sits down on the floor, pulls the game out, and places it on the coffee table.

His dog Atticus lies down right beside him, putting his head in Jake's lap, looking quite content to lie there for a while.

I sit down on the floor between the couch and the coffee table, letting my leg stretch on the floor beside the coffee table. This allows me to rest and stretch out my legs.

"Is this okay? We can move to the desk if you want," Jake says, his face full of concern.

"You might have to help me up off the floor when we are done, but I am comfortable."

Jake sets up the board game, and we go over the rules to refresh our memory before we play.

"Of all the branches, what made you pick the Army?" he asks after we both had our first turn in the game.

"My grandfather was in the Army back in the Korean War. I guess it was a small way to honor him but where I also felt I'd be the most useful," I shrug, not really wanting to get into it. "Why did you pick the Navy?"

"Because the Navy Seals are the best." He smiles at me, but there's just a hint of mischief in his beautiful brown eyes.

We go through a few rounds of the game while we talk about previous times we played. Caden could never get the concept of how to win the games, especially Monopoly. Half the time when he would play, he would get so frustrated he'd flip the board and walk away.

Even though Caden would get upset about it, I just laughed. And secretly, I would look forward to him flipping the board. There was just something so comfortable about how competitive he was. I'm assuming that competitive streak has only grown.

"How are your brothers doing?" I ask, wanting to keep the conversation light.

He tenses, looking up at me, studying me for a moment.

"I'm not asking to get information about Caden. Playing makes me miss the times we would all sit together, and I'm just wondering what they are doing."

He relaxes just a bit before taking his next turn.

"Caden joined the Marines and is doing some training right now. I haven't heard from him in a while. Brantley is currently deployed with the Marines as well. North joined the Navy like I did but decided against applying to be a Seal."

"How does your mom feel about having all four of her boys in the military?"

"Some days, she's a nervous wreck, but in general, she's just proud," he says with a smile. Though that smile was forced, and there's something else there. I want to ask him about it, but asking him to open up means that I would have to open up, and that's not going to happen.

We play a little bit longer, and he talks about his brothers, how he was able to be at each of their boot camp graduations, and how proud he is of them. It starts to feel like old times. Then, there's a break in the conversation.

"When I was healing after I came back Stateside, I really wish there had been a place like Oakside for me. It sure as hell beats any hospital room I stayed in," he says, looking around. I start to get uncomfortable. Not because he's here but because I see where the conversation is going.

"When I was healing, I felt so alone. My mom was there, but my entire unit was still deployed. North was the only one who was able to come to visit because Brantley and Caden were deployed. And I hadn't really made friends outside of my unit. Took me a long time to find the right people to surround myself with. No, I couldn't imagine not having Noah and Easton and some of the other guys here," he says.

"If I had had a place like this, who knows where I'd be? The therapist that worked with Dr. Tate at the hospital could never remember my name and kept getting my story mixed up with another patient."

That's when it clicks, and the anger starts to boil deep in my guts.

"Who was it that told you to come and talk to me? Noah or Dr. Tate himself?" I ask through clenched teeth.

Jake's eyes go wide, "That's not it. I was just going down memory lane. Shit! I'm sorry. Let's just go back to safer topics."

"I think you should go," I say, pulling myself up with sheer arm strength and throwing myself back up onto the couch.

Jake hesitates for only a moment before he nods and starts packing up the game. When he stands, he sets the game on my desk.

"I'm going to leave this here in case you want to play even if it's not with me," he says, sadness in his voice that somehow grips my heart in a way that I don't quite understand.

That emotion is new and raw and not something I want to deal with right now.

"I will check in on you in a few days," he says, walking towards the door.

"Don't bother," I say to his back, and he pauses at the door, then leaves.

I pick up my tablet and start reading again, lost in the world that won't let me down. Reading the same page over and over without actually seeing the words, trying to make sense of why it hurts so much to find out that he wasn't here to actually spend time with me, but because someone sent him.

I don't know how long I sit there reading the same page when there's another knock on my door.

Lexi's voice fills the room. "Don't be mad at him. He was just trying to help. We are all worried about you."

Without looking up or even acknowledging, I wait for her to leave. But this time, when I try to read the page, the words actually start to register.

Back to my morally gray men who make questionable decisions because they actually love the woman, not because they feel obligated to help out their brother's ex.

Chapter 5

Jake

Today, I have off work, but Atticus and I have a super-secret mission that we're on. The way that things ended with Kassi the other day is not sitting right with me. So, I've been racking my brain on how to make things right.

After stopping at her favorite burger place in town, I got a burger surprise and a milkshake for both her and me. Now my top secret mission is to smuggle it into Oakside.

Don't get me wrong, Oakside has some delicious food, and they have a skilled chef in the kitchen. But the food is all healthy, and I know when I was in recovery, I would have given anything for a greasy burger and fries. Don't get me started on a milkshake.

Working at Oakside has its benefits. I know all the best ways to sneak by and not get caught by Noah, Lexi, or Easton.

A few of the volunteers spot me, smiling and shaking their heads, but I know they won't rat me out. Heading straight to Kassi's room, thankfully, I find her there on the couch reading, just like the last time I was here.

Once Atticus and I are in her room, I close the door behind me, which catches her attention. She looks up at me and scowls, but I don't blame her.

"I come with a peace offering," I say, holding up the food and drinks.

Her expression softens, and she sets the tablet down on the coffee table.

Going over to the coffee table, I put down the food. "Burger, fries, and a milkshake. All things I was craving but couldn't have during my recovery." Then I sit in the same spot on the floor, using the coffee table to hold our food.

Like she did last time, she slides down onto the floor between the couch and the coffee table.

"Thank you for this," she says with a soft smile.

That smile does funny things to my heart, and suddenly, my mind is racing with ways to put more smiles on her face. It's an emotion I don't quite understand.

"I hate how we left things, and I really am sorry. Yes, I was told that you weren't talking, and yes, I suggested that maybe you talking to me might help. But I'm not here to force you to talk about whatever it is you don't want to talk about. I'm here as your friend because I care about you." I give her the speech I practiced in the car on the way here.

She opens the burger in front of her but doesn't touch it. Then she looks up at me, her eyes studying my face. However, she doesn't respond right away.

When her eyes roam over me, it's as if she's actually touching me. My heart races as she studies me. Then something clicks into place, and one word runs through my head.

Mine.

It catches me completely off guard. I push that thought aside to unpack later.

"Friends, huh?" she smiles and tilts her head, picking up her burger and taking a bite.

There's something about the way she said it that I'm not sure how to react or what to say next. Instead, I watch her in silence for a few minutes.

"I've always wondered how boot camp was different for the Army compared to the Navy," I muse.

Smirking, she says, "I guess, in most ways, the same. Lots of yelling, waking you up in the middle of the night, punishments if you don't do things right."

"How many did you have drop out of boot camp?" I ask.

"Ten that I know of. I was the only female to graduate with my class."

She says it like it's no big deal, but it is a huge deal. That's a major accomplishment. But right now doesn't feel like the time to say it, so I remain silent. Nevertheless, I really am proud of her for it.

"I only know of six that dropped out when I went to boot camp. They did say we had one of the smaller units at the time," I tell her.

While we enjoy your burgers, we continue to compare our experiences at boot camp. The conversation flows and is easy.

"Did you guys have to do the gas chamber?" I ask her, remembering an exercise that caused us to lose three people in a day.

"Oh my God, yes! We had two people that refused to do it and packed their bags that day. It was so bad many of us were sick after, but we still cleaned our barracks and the bathrooms," she says, laughing.

It's one of those things when you share experiences that were hard and took everything out of you at the time, but now you can look back and laugh at it.

Even more so, it bonds you in a way that people who've never been through it just won't understand. Doesn't matter what branch of the military you're in, boot camp and the shared experiences of deployment injuries unites you. Sometimes those bonds run deeper than people you've known your whole life.

As we continue to talk, it's nice to see her loosen up and smile. We tell stories from our boot camp and training days about the people we met and the ways we got into trouble.

I find myself trying to make her smile more because she is stunningly beautiful when she smiles. This leads to me telling her the most ridiculous stories from my service time. Though in order not to upset her, I avoid all mentions of deployments.

When I look at my watch, I realize we have been talking for almost three hours, and I really should leave her to read her book before dinner.

"I should get going and let you get back to reading."

When I stand to clean up our mess at the table, I swear I see disappointment cross her face before she masks it. Though maybe I'm imagining things because I don't want to leave.

Walking to her, I offer my hand to help her up off the floor since she can't put weight on one of her legs. She hesitates for only a moment before taking my hand. The sparks from something as simple as taking her hand catch me off guard.

Judging by her sharp intake of breath, she felt it, too. As I help her up, the momentum pulls her into my chest. Once she is standing, we both freeze. There is no way she doesn't feel how hard I am from just having her near.

Watching her reaction, I notice how her eyes run over my face before they land on my lips. Fuck. She has to stop looking at me like that. I'm about to take a step back when her tongue comes out and licks her lips. It's then I know I'm totally fucked.

I can't not kiss her now. Like a moth to a flame, I lean in slowly, and her eyes go wide. What I see there isn't shock, it's desire, which spurs me on. My lips land on hers, and the moan she lets out seals her fate. She is mine even when I know she can't be. Doesn't matter to me at the moment. Even though I know I can't have her, there isn't a way in hell I'm walking away either.

Wrapping an arm around her waist, I pull her to me. She rests her hands on my shoulders, and I deepen the kiss, memorizing her soft lips on mine. Pulling her even closer to me, I run my tongue along the seam of her mouth. When she opens for me and our tongues meet, cum leaks from my cock.

I've never had this kind of reaction to a girl before. Fuck. Why does it have to be with the one girl I can't have?

Atticus nudges my hip, pushing his head between us, bringing us both back to reality. Releasing her, I stare at her just kissed lips, and my cock gets even harder, knowing I'm the reason they are swollen.

"Fuck, we shouldn't have done that," I say, running a hand through my hair.

Hurt flickers in her eyes and no way am I letting her mind run down that road. Bending slightly, I look into her eyes and place my hand on her shoulders.

"But I'm glad we did." At my words, a smile fills her face.

Then, I gently help her sit on the couch.

"Can I come by tomorrow and maybe try playing Payday again?" I ask.

"I'd like that," she says.

Relief hits me.

We say our goodbyes and I head outside to get some fresh air. What the hell just happened?

Chapter 6

Kassi

I can't concentrate on anything since Jake kissed me yesterday. It was like a book boyfriend's kiss would be. The only difference is I experienced it in real life, and it was so much better than any of the books I've read.

What is wrong with me?

I kissed my ex-boyfriend's older brother!

Not only that, but it was also the best kiss of my damn life. The sparks from our hands touching and the way he looked at me were off the charts hot. The worst part is I'm not sorry, and I know when I see him again, I will want to do it again. And I wouldn't stop him if he leaned in and kissed me.

Do guys have the same code as girls? Like, his brother dated me, so am I off limits? The last thing I want to do is break his family apart. They have always been so close, which I always loved about them.

Crap, I don't know what to do, and I don't have anyone to talk to.

"Hey, you, okay? You look pretty far up in your head," my nurse, Kaitlyn, asks.

She has been super sweet, and I feel bad about how I treated her when I first met her.

"When I joined the military, I lost a lot of my friends who didn't understand why I'd join," I tell her. Though I had never been a girly girl, and they just didn't get it. But man, I'd kill for a friend to talk to right now." I don't know why I tell her that, but I do. It's like I need to get it out.

She looks at me for a minute, then out the window.

"I have an idea. Give me a few minutes to see if I can make it happen," she says before turning and leaving my room. Since I don't have anything else to go on, I simply shrug and wait. I have no idea what to expect.

A little while later, Lexi comes to my door, knocking on the door frame.

"Hey, can I come in?" she asks.

I like how she always asks, so I nod. After entering and sitting in my comfy oversized chair, she says, "Kaitlyn told me what you said. We don't normally do this with patients, but you and Jake have a history, and Jake is one of us. Anyway, the girls do a very informal girls' night once or twice a month at my place. We eat food, those who can drink, and we talk about everything and anything. There is no judgment, and nothing leaves the room. We are having one tonight, and you should come," she encourages.

I get a sinking feeling it wasn't a planned girls' night and that it was put together for me. Other than Lexi, I would be meeting a bunch of strangers. I don't know how comfortable I'd be.

"I don't know. I wouldn't know anyone," I say.

"Well, you kind of would. It would be me, Paisley, who is Easton's wife. Mandy, she works here. You met her a few times. Kaitlyn, who you know, and Lauren and Faith, who both work here but haven't worked with you yet. Also, there will be one other nurse, Brooke. Anything you say will stay in the cone of silence, and when you come back here, you will have a base of people you can talk to when you need to. I already cleared it with them. They are all excited to meet you, officially," she says with a huge smile.

"You should do it. We have a ton of fun, and you won't be the only one sharing. Then we talk gossip about whatever we need to get off our chest and to be stress free. Our guys normally hang out in the backyard, have a beer, and grill some food. It's a good time, and we have fun. Plus, it is cathartic," Kaitlyn says walking back into my room from the hallway.

Silently, I think it over. I do like Lexi and Kaitlyn. They are both super nice, and boy, I could use some advice.

"Okay, I guess," I say hesitantly.

"Yay! Noah and I will come and get you soon. We have a golf cart to get us over to our place. It's just next door." She points toward the tree on the side of the property. "The walking path there actually leads to our house, and we have an open-door policy if anyone ever needs to talk to us," she says.

Though I can't help wondering how she feels about living next door to where she works and how many patients wander over.

"See you soon," she says, leaving me to ponder just how much I actually want to tell them.

***

I'm standing in Lexi's kitchen and meeting all the girls' husbands. Yep, husbands, because apparently, I will be the only single one here tonight. These guys all seem to be straight out of a book. They are very attentive to their girls, protective, and are always watching them, even from across the room. Someone might try to say it's a red flag, but when I see the love on their faces, I know it's genuine. Like now, Kaitlyn slides up to her husband Grayson's side, and he wraps her in a hug. She gets his full attention. It's so damn sweet, and it's what I want.

As everyone is talking about the band *Highway 55* coming in to play for us in a few weeks, I'm still at the door with a smile on my face.

"Hey, I was beginning to think you weren't coming!" Paisley exclaims, rushing toward the door to greet me enthusiastically.

When he enters the kitchen, Jake is immediately at her side but stops short when he sees me. Our eyes lock, and the room becomes quiet. After looking around, he gives me a tight smile before walking up to my side.

"What are you doing here?" I ask lamely.

"I suspect the same thing you are," he says, grabbing one of the little sausages wrapped in bacon that Lexi made.

"Well, let's get this party started!" Lexi claps her hands to get our attention. "We will be in the sunroom, and it's a no-boys area. Guys are out back, and no girls are allowed there either. If you need to talk to your man, you do it here in the kitchen or living room. Let's go!"

Then Lexi hurries to me and walks with me as she helps me navigate her house on crutches.

The sunroom almost feels like we are in an entirely different house. What I've seen of the house so far, is it's done with a rustic farmhouse feel using lots of grays and blues. Out here in the sunroom, it has more of a bohemian vibe with bright colors, plants, fairy lights, and even a few swings in the corners of the room.

"Okay, listen up. Girls' night rules," Lexi says and holds up a finger. "One, no drinking and driving. There are guest bedrooms upstairs and downstairs and couches around the house. Crash anywhere. You are always welcome."

She holds up a second finger. "Two, we are friends first. We are not bosses and employees. We are not nurses and patients, we are friends, and we are here as friends. Venting about work is okay. Venting about patients is okay. Venting about guys is encouraged. We are here to support each other," she says.

Then she holds up a third finger, "Three. What is talked about at girls' night stays at girls' night. This is a safe place. What is talked about in this room doesn't leave this room. Got it?"

We all agree before digging into the food she's put on the coffee table in the middle of the room. Lexi fills my plate for me and brings it over so I don't have to get up. There is another table with water, soda, tea, and alcoholic drinks. Judging by the setup, it looks like this is something they do often.

"I really need to get those rules made into a sign and put them on the wall somewhere in here," Lexi says.

"She says them every time, and I think we can all repeat it word for word now," Kaitlyn says, sitting down next to me.

As we eat taco salad and chicken sliders with sides like potato salad and coleslaw, I eye the brownies for dessert. The food is so good, and a nice break from what we get at Oakside.

Lauren kicks the night off by talking about her son and how he got into a fight at school this week. Apparently, some kids were teasing him, saying his dad wasn't his real dad because he wasn't there when he was born. I guess Lauren and her husband were high school sweethearts, and he broke up with her when he enlisted, and she found out afterward that she was pregnant. They met again here at Oakside and fell in love all over again before Gavin even found out he had a son.

At least, that's what Kaitlyn fills me in on as Lauren is talking.

"Well, I will go next," Kaitlyn always beside me.

"My dad introduced me to a woman he has been seeing. He brought her to family dinner the other night," she says, turning to me. "A few years ago, Dad divorced my stepmom and moved here to be with me and Grayson. He's been single, and I had no idea he was even seeing anyone."

"What did you think of her?" Lexi asks, and everyone is quiet.

"I don't know. What I don't want to do is let my fear of what his last wife did cloud my judgment. This woman was nice but shy, like she was scared of me or Grayson. So, I simply don't know." She looks down at her plate.

"My guess is he told her what happened before, so she's just as nervous as you. I'm sure your dad is too. Just get to know her and call a girls' night if you need to work it out," Mandy says from the other side of her as she pulls her in for a hug.

Lexi catches my eye and smiles, but no one forces me to talk. As the night goes on, I get more comfortable and decide I really need to get this off my chest.

"I guess it's my turn," I say at the next conversation break.

"You all know Jake," I say, since he's here tonight. They all nod, so I take a deep breath.

"Well, I've known him since we were in school. I dated his younger brother, Caden, in high school. Not long after Jake left for boot camp, we broke up. I hadn't seen him or talked to anyone in his family until I ran into him here at Oakside." I stop to take a sip of water, suddenly wishing it was something stronger. Because of the pain meds I'm on, I can't have any alcohol right now when I need some liquid courage. Fortunately, I don't have much pain, but I might need one tonight after such a long outing.

"Yesterday, he came to my room, and we talked and played board games like old times. But when he was getting ready to leave, he helped me back to the sofa, and something shifted, and we..." Good lord, I can't even bring myself to say it. "We kissed," I say really fast and then look down at my now empty plate.

"How did you feel about the kiss?" Lexi asks softly.

"It was the best damn kiss of my life," I cringe.

The entire room erupts in hoots and hollers, and I can't help but laugh and smile at them.

"So, the holdup is that you dated his brother?" Kaitlyn asks.

"Yeah, and I don't want to break up their family or cause any trouble. They are so close, and that's one of the things I always loved when I was with them."

"Jake is a grown man, and you have to let him make that choice. It's his family," Lexi says.

"You know, my husband Levi was my best friend's ex-boyfriend," Mandy says.

"I get it," she goes on. "There was this wall there. I knew I shouldn't be feeling the way I did, but I couldn't stop it. When he was dating her, I never felt those feelings. We were just friends. But Levi, as an adult, I don't know something changed," Mandy says.

"Yes!" I say. "When I was dating his brother, I never had feelings for him outside of being his friend. But seeing him now as an adult, it's like he's a different person but still the same in a lot of ways."

Turning to Mandy, I ask "How did it work out for you? Obviously, you are married, but how did your friend find out?"

"At first, I went through stages of guilt and even anger. Even though she was married to another man, I felt guilty. Then I was like fuck that, she's married. She has no claim on him. Eventually, when she found out, she was pretty angry. I was mad that she was mad, and then I was hurt. But honestly, it was Levi who smoothed it all out. It's still a little weird sometimes, like at the wedding, but otherwise she's still my friend."

I nod, taking it all in.

"If I could do one thing differently?" Mandy interjects, "I would have been honest and open to Levi sooner about how I felt. He didn't see it as a problem because they broke up, but he was worried about how it would affect me and didn't say anything. You should talk to him when you see him at Oakside. He was in your shoes."

"This is all, of course, if you even want something more than just that kiss," Lexi says softly.

Do I want more? I've been imagining more all night, but do I really want more?

"Yeah, I think I do want more," I smile.

Chapter 7

Jake

It's been a few days since our first kiss and then seeing Kassi at Lexi's house. Even though I was surprised to see her, I was glad she was there. Not only were there all kinds of things swirling around in my head, but I had friends that I could talk to which helped tremendously. I'm sure she needed an outlet, too.

It's taken everything in me not to ask Lexi what happened and what was talked about.

Kassi got her cast off yesterday, which means no more crutches, so she's added physical therapy to her appointment list. Sadly, they couldn't be scheduled in the mornings, but instead, they were after lunch. But regardless, we still have plenty of time to see each other.

There have been more kisses, but it hasn't really gone any further than that, even though I'm pretty sure we both wanted to. When I'm not with her, I can't seem to get our kisses out of my head.

I've never experienced kissing the way that she kisses me. The sounds alone that she makes have me harder than I think I've ever been in my life. My hand is just not enough to satisfy me anymore, but I won't ever push her for more.

"Jake!" Easton says, getting my attention. Fortunately, it pulls me out of my head and from spiraling down the path of what Kassi would be like under me.

"Sorry," I say, trying to focus on him. We are at work, after all.

"Everything okay?" He asks, watching me closely.

"Yeah, I'm fine." I don't want to get into it with a few of the volunteers around here who are listening in.

He studies me for a minute, and it's like he knows exactly what I'm thinking because he sends the other guys away until it's just him, Noah, and me.

"Is this about more of what we talked about the other night at my place?" Noah asks.

That night that we had dinner at his place and the girls had their girls' night, I eventually broke down and told the guys what was going on. I laid it all out about how she dated my brother, about how I didn't have feelings for her then, but I definitely have feelings for her now.

Then I told him about the earth-shattering kiss. They made a good point, telling me I needed to talk to my brother. But the problem is, I can't get hold of him. It's not that he's not answering. His phone is off, so he won't even know that he had a missed call from me. Though I've only called once.

"Yeah, I tried to call my brother, but he didn't answer. His phone is off, so I guess he's at training or something. But that hasn't stopped me from seeing her every day. There have been more kisses, but it hasn't gone further than that, though I'm pretty sure we both want it to."

"What's holding you back?" Easton asks.

"Well, for one thing, I can't get ahold of my brother. Also, I don't want her to think that's all I want from her. And if I'm being really honest, just my own fear," I tell them.

"So, take her on a date," Noah says it like it's the simplest thing in the world.

"Talk to Lexi. She can help you set something up here. When I was trying to do the same thing for Paisley, she was a great help," Easton says, reading my mind before I could even voice it.

"She's in her office. Go talk to her," Noah urges.

Without really giving me a choice, they walk me down to her office. Noah strides right over to her. She's sitting at her desk, and he pulls her up, and in one swift movement, he's in her chair, and she's on his lap.

"Jake needs your help, Angel. He wants to plan a date here for Kassi," he tells her.

Her eyes snap to mine. "I have the perfect idea for dinner tonight. I'll handle the details. You just get her to agree," Lexi says, beaming at me with her eyes sparkling.

"Thank you," I say.

Noah whispers something in her ear before she looks back up at me.

"I'm not going to betray her trust, but I will tell you this: you've really got to get the situation with your brother figured out, or there's no point in moving forward." She tells me this with a sad smile, and my heart sinks.

"I'm trying. I think he's in training right now. His phone must be turned off," I tell her. What I don't say is that I've only tried one time to call, and I'm terrified and acting like a coward by not trying again.

"Okay, well, you've got to get her to agree to tonight, so off you go," she says.

I'm getting ready to head upstairs when I run into Dr. Tate.

"Oh, Jake. Thank you for spending some time with Kassi. You don't have to tell me what you said or what you two talked about, but she's finally starting to open up. She's talking and answering questions, and she's making amazing progress. I have to thank you for that," he says, placing a hand on my shoulder.

While I'm happy she's finally opening up, finally talking, and finally healing, I hate that he thinks it's because of me. Because part of me knows this is all going to blow up in my face, and when it does, I don't want her to blame me for one more thing.

"Well, I'm glad, though I don't think I can take credit for that. You don't have to thank me for being there for her. I would have done it regardless. You have to give yourself some credit," I tell him, hoping he'll understand.

Thankfully, he doesn't push it but heads into Lexi's office as I go upstairs.

I find Kassi on the couch, reading just like I knew I would. Though I tap on her door frame, I don't step foot inside her room because, technically, I'm still working.

When she looks up and sees me, her face lights up in a heart-stopping smile.

"Jake," she sighs, like I'm her salvation, and that alone has me getting hard. Fuck, in all honesty, just being around this girl has me hard.

"Do you have any plans tonight?" I ask, not budging from the doorway.

"I don't know. Let me check my super busy social calendar. Since you probably know this already, Oakside has such a huge social scene." She smirks while glancing down at the tablet in her hands. "Well, look at that. I happen to be free tonight."

I love her sass and the fact that it's starting to come back, proving she's on the mend.

"Well, dress up. I'm taking you on a date. See you at six," I say. Then I turn around to leave before she can ask me, I'm sure, the millions of questions that she's going to have.

None of which I have the answers to.

***

I've been pacing in the lobby for forty-five minutes, not wanting to show up too early to get her. It's now ten minutes to six.

"Fuck it," I mutter under my breath and head down the hallway to go pick her up.

Her door is closed, and when I knock, I can hear her shuffling around. She opens the door, and my jaw hits the ground.

When you're in recovery, having clothes for a special event is not exactly a priority, so I was just expecting jeans and a nice shirt. What I was not expecting was the stunning maxi dress that she has on. Not only does it hug her curves in all the right places, it makes her breasts the center of my attention.

Her makeup is done, accentuating her beautiful eyes and her plump, tempting lips. All I want right now is to kiss her. She took the time to curl her hair, and it falls perfectly around her pretty face.

"I... You... Wow," is all I'm able to get out because my brain seems to be malfunctioning.

"You look pretty good there yourself, soldier," she says with a smile, taking in my dark jeans and button-down shirt.

"Well," I say, still taking her in. "I don't think there is a word for how beautiful you look right now. Beautiful isn't even strong enough of a word, stunning, magnificent, perfect."

Mine.

I wonder how she'd react to that last one because that one seems to be the only one able to encompass my current feelings.

When I hold my hand out to her, she takes it with a smile on her face.

Slowly, we make our way out to the front porch and then to the garden, which Lexi has closed off this evening just for us.

Stone walls covered in ivy and flowers surround the garden. It gives the patient here the ability to escape reality and forget where they are. Many find it a great hiding space.

There are swings, benches, pathways, flowers, herbs, and trees. I take her to the back corner of the garden, where there's a small waterfall and where Lexi has set up a picnic dinner for us.

When she sees it, she stops and looks up at me with her jaw open.

"You did this?" She whispers in shock.

"I had a little help," I admit with a smile. I lead her over to the blankets that are spread on the ground, and we both take a seat.

We sit, eat, and talk. It's not the typical first date talk because, let's face it, we know each other way better than most people who are on a first date. We share about everything from TV shows we like watch to places we still want to visit.

Touching on our childhoods and our time in high school brings back so many memories. We went to the same high school, but we weren't in the same grade, so we did have different experiences. We talk about our reasons for joining the military and our plans and hopes for what to do beyond the military.

After we are finished eating, we put everything back into the basket that Lexi had set it in. She even included some treats for Atticus, who has been lying next to the water like he's on some tropical vacation.

Then I maneuver her so she's sitting between my legs, resting her back on my chest. With us not being face to face, it makes some of the harder topics easier, and the mood shifts.

"Have you talked to Caden?" she asks, resting her head on my shoulder as I wrap my arms around her waist.

"I tried to call him, but his phone was shut off. That means he's usually in training. I'll try again in a few days." I tell her, kissing her temple.

She nods her head and nothing else is said for a while as we sit in comfortable silence. If I want her to open up to me, I know I need to open up to her, but this doesn't seem like the time or the place.

Chapter 8

Kassi

S itting there with Jake's arms around me was like something out of a movie. Talking and sharing about ourselves with each other was what I needed. I didn't know that I was longing for a deeper connection, and this time with him provided it.

We stayed there until well after dark. When the garden lit up with fairy lights and made it look magical, I was transported to a secret fairy garden. I didn't want to leave.

Once we packed everything up, we walked hand in hand around the garden and back up to Oakside. And now we are standing outside my door, and things are awkward.

I don't want the night to end. It's been so perfect. But I don't know if he is feeling the same way or if maybe it was a bust and I didn't live up to what he had in his head. I simply don't know, and it's the not knowing I don't like.

Leaning against my closed door, I look up at him, hoping I can see in his gaze what he is thinking. Though he doesn't say anything, but I wish with all my heart that he would. He's still holding my hand, and he looks down at it, rubbing his thumb over my knuckles. The sensation sends tingles down my spine.

Then he looks back up at me.

"You feel that too, right?" he whispers. To make his point, he again runs his thumb over my knuckles, and sure enough, the same electric zing hits me.

I nod my head because it feels impossible to get words out. His eyes flit down to my lips, and that is the only warning I get before his lips crash into mine. When I kiss him back, it's like all bets are off, and he backs me up, so my back is to my door, and I'm pressed up against him.

It begins like our other kisses, but before long, there is so much more passion and longing in it. Maybe because we already knew each other or because we're spending more time together, but this kiss is powerful and intense. Soul shattering. Atticus breaks the moment by nudging his head between our legs, and Jake pulls back enough to whisper against my lips.

"We should take this into your room and not do this in the hallway," he says, reaching around me and opening the door.

Stumbling into the room, not wanting to let each other go, Jake holds me tight around my waist. Once Atticus is in, he closes the door and presses me back against it.

"Atticus, go lay down," he says, and the dog immediately jumps on the couch and lies down. From there Atticus has a perfect view of the entire room and of course, us.

I open my mouth to ask if he needs some food or water, but Jake's lips are back on mine again before I can get any words out.

His warm, firm lips are kissing me, and his arms run down my sides, gripping my ass, pulling me towards him even closer until I can feel his heart beating. Then he pulls my leg up giving him better access to my already wet core. When he grinds himself into me, I can feel the hardness of his cock. How hard he is for *me*.

Restlessly, I move, trying to get pressure where I need it most. I'm on fire, my body is trembling, and I'm so close to exploding just from the kissing and the little touching we've been doing. As I move, attempting to get him where I want some relief, he lets out a long groan that is sexy as hell.

Then he picks me up, so I wrap my legs around his waist as he carries me to the bed and gently sets me down all without his lips leaving mine.

"If you don't want this, you need to stop me now," he whispers as he glides his lips down my neck.

There is no way I'm stopping this, no universe where I say I don't want him. Without words, I wrap my arms around his neck and pull him into me.

"Don't stop," I breathe.

"Fuck," he mutters before turning and going toward the door.

My heart sinks. Well, at least he had more self-control than I did. When he reaches it, he locks it and comes back to me.

Not wasting a minute, his lips crash onto mine again. When he reaches for my dress, he hesitates, like he's waiting for me to tell him no or change my mind. Eagerly, I help him by lifting my arms up in a silent acknowledgment. He looks into my eyes, and the desire on his face is not something I've ever experienced. It makes me even hotter to see how much he wants me.

A moment later, my dress is gone and on the floor. When I reach for his shirt, eager to see his muscular chest, he tenses before ripping it off. Standing in front of me, he's breathing heavily, and he lets me gaze at his magnificent upper body. Wow, it doesn't disappoint! The first thing that I see is the black ink tattoos on his upper arms and chest, and scattered around them are the scars. Some of the scars are clean cut, and some are jagged.

I reach out and trace a few of them, realizing I know nothing of his story, and I suddenly want to, but there's no way in hell I'm stopping this to ask. So I pull him back to kiss me some more. Urgently, like I'll die if he stops.

But the spell is broken when he puts me on the bed and crawls in after me. Reaching behind my back, his large hands unhook my bra, which joins the other clothes on the floor.

"You are so beautiful," he mutters. Then, his heated mouth teases along my neck, making me hold my breath in anticipation. When his kiss lands on my collarbone, then behind my ear and the hollow of my throat, it ignites a fire deep in me. I want more. Much more.

Taking one of my nipples into his mouth, he worships me with his tongue.

The gentleness of his tongue, combined with the hard sucking, causes a bolt of pleasure to shoot through my body. After giving my other breasts the same devoted attention, he moves his glorious lips kissing down to my stomach and stops at the waistband of my panties.

He pauses, looking up at me for permission. Quickly, I nod because holy hell, that last thing I want him to do is stop. He slides my panties slowly down my legs. Judging by his sharp intake of breath and the bulge behind his boxers, he likes what he sees. Finally, he stands, taking all of me in, and I let him boldly look at me. Our eyes lock, and my body is on fire, ready to go. He pulls off his boxer briefs, and his very large, very wide, very erect cock springs out. While I'm gazing at him in awe, he lets out a string of curses. "I don't have a condom," he says.

I can't help but laugh.

"Check the nightstand. Lexi dropped some off this morning, and I couldn't for the life of me figure out why, but I get it now," I tell him.

With relief written all over his face, he quickly moves towards the nightstand. He rolls the condom on at record speed before climbing into bed with me.

Caging me and resting on his elbows, while keeping his weight off of me, makes me feel safe. I never understood why girls loved this position so much, but I get it now, this feeling of security. It's as if he's protecting me from the rest of the world.

Then I hear some shifting over on the couch and I remember Atticus.

"What about Atticus?" I ask, suddenly nervous about a dog watching us.

He looks over his shoulder for a moment and then shifts, pulling the blankets over us.

"He'll be asleep in a minute anyway," Jake says before leaning in to kiss me and tracing his fingers over my belly down to my clit where he gently rubs me. Even from this slightest touch, I can feel the wetness surge between legs causing me to tremble. He can feel how soaking wet I am. This time his moan matches mine.

"Baby, you are soaked," he smirks.

"I always am around you." I pull him back down for another breathtaking kiss.

"Fuck," he whispers against my lips.

His fingers continue to work their magic, sending ripples of pleasure throughout my body. With his lips on mine in a passionate kiss, I feel his hard cock pressed against me, fully erect and eager to be inside me.

Jake pulls away slightly, his eyes locked on mine, conveying the intensity of his desire. "Are you ready?" he asks, his voice low and rough.

Unable to speak, I nod, wrapping my legs around his waist, pulling him closer to me. He positions himself at my entrance, teasing me with the slightest pressure before slowly sliding inside me. I gasp, my head falling back as the sensation washes over me.

What I'm experiencing is unlike anything I've ever known. It's a perfect mix of pleasure and pain as his long thickness fills me completely.

"God, you feel so good," he murmurs, kissing my neck as he moves inside me.

He thrusts slowly at first, watching me as I arch my back and cry out with every stroke. The feeling intensifies, and by the rapid rhythm of his breaths in my ear, he's as in tune with the moment as I am.

Suddenly, he pulls out and flips me onto my hands and knees. He enters me from behind, gripping my hips and pounding into me, his movements growing more urgent.

"You feel so good, so tight. Your ass is perfect," he growls in my ear as he continues to move within me. "I can't make this last much longer the way your pussy is clenching around me."

I turn my head to look over my shoulder and see him watching me with a mix of desire and wonder in his eyes. "Good, because I don't want to stop either!"

He reaches around to play with my clit, causing me to cry out and buck against him, the exquisite sensation sending me spiraling towards an orgasm.

His thrusts become more frantic, as he plunged deeper and deeper. "Come for me, baby," he growls.

That's all it takes. With a loud cry into the pillow, I shatter into pieces, waves of pleasure washing over me as Jake continues to thrust inside me.

"Fuck," he groans, his voice hoarse with desire. He slams into me one last time as he finds his release.

We lay there, panting and entwined, our bodies still connected. "That was..." I start searching for the right words.

"Amazing," Jake completes the sentence, still catching his breath.

I have to laugh. "I was going to say perfect, but I guess amazing works, too."

He kisses my neck gently, his heartbeat slowing down. "It was perfect. And I've never felt anything like that before in my life."

I stroke his hair, still amazed he's here with me. With one more gentle kiss, then he is up and in the bathroom. A moment later, he is back, the condom gone and a washcloth in his hand. He gently cleans between my legs before tossing it back in the bathroom and lying down with me.

When he pulls me into his arms and holds me tight, I've never felt so safe. I love the feel of his solid warrior's body against me, and I snuggle to him with my head on his arm. After a minute, he turns me so my head is on his chest.

When I notice a scar on his side in the shape of a crescent moon, I trace it gently. The scar is a part of him, and I wonder about the story behind it.

As if reading my mind, he says, "I can't talk about a lot of what happened to me. Not because I don't want to, but because it's still classified. What I can tell you is I was in a Seal Team, and we had some dangerous missions and saw some horrible things.

Many times, we couldn't interfere, and that's what killed me. We couldn't stop grown men from raping little girls while the whole village watched. Anyone who interfered was killed on the spot. That is the stuff that still haunts me. Not my kill count, not the men we lost, but that I couldn't stop the men from hurting the women and children."

"Jake, that's horrible. It's not a part of war many people think about or even want to think about, but it happens so often. I'm sorry you had to witness that."

"It's why I have Atticus. Sometimes, the memories get so strong, and it gets hard to pull myself out. He knows when it's happening, and he's there for me. Since I've been working here helping people out, it's happened less frequently."

"I guess that helping people here offsets what you couldn't do there," I say, making the connection, and he just nods.

"The scars are from a building that was bombed. I didn't lose anyone, but I ended up injured by flying debris. After everything, that is what got me medically discharged. And by then, I was more than ready to be done."

He opened up to me, and I know he's never pushed me, but I feel like I should thank him for it by giving him a part of me. And I very much want to.

"I was..." Taking a deep breath, I'm not sure what I want to say. But I decide to go for it. "I was stationed at a field hospital. After patients were injured, we got them stabilized so they could be transferred out. We saw a lot of gruesome things, but we saved so many people that came to us, we had an excellent track record. When we could, we sent medical supplies into villages."

Jake holds me tighter but doesn't say anything.

"I guess we gained a reputation. In the last deployment, we had to move the hospital twice because our location was compromised. We had a few guys transferring out that morning with an escort, and my patient and I had been talking. He knew a few people I was in boot camp with, so it was a fun time for us to catch up. I lost track of time and wasn't where I was supposed to be when we were bombed. I was safe on the other side of the base. He and I both ran to help, and... We lost so many people that day, and I should have been one of them." I say the words that have been circling my head.

In an instant, he has me flipped onto my back and pinned to the bed.

"Don't say that! You were exactly where you were supposed to be. The Universe kept you there for a reason. It wasn't your time. How many did you save while you were still injured?" he asks.

"Five, before a beam fell, crushing my leg," I choke out as my eyes burns.

"If you weren't on the other side of the base, those five would have died, too. You wouldn't be here at Oakside, and I wouldn't have found the person I was missing. I wouldn't have fallen for you," he whispers.

Even if I tried, I can't stop the tears. He leans in and gently kisses them away.

"I get the guilt. I wish I could say it will go away, but I'm not sure it completely does. We just learn to live with it. You still get nightmares?" he asks.

I just nod.

"Me too," he says.

He lies back down and pulls me in tight to his side. If there is one person who knows what I'm feeling, it's Jake.

I just need to let him in.

Chapter 9

Jake

I screwed up. I shouldn't have slept with Kassi before I got a chance to talk to my brother. I don't regret it for one moment, but yesterday it made me realize that I have fallen in love with her.

Then, of course, I had to go tell her. But her story ripped my heart out. I can't even think about her not being here with me. I'd lose my goddamned mind. Taking a deep breath, I try to call my brother again. It doesn't ring but goes straight to voicemail.

Fuck.

Instead, I do the next best thing and get in the car to talk to my mom. She has good and bad days, so she needs more care now. My brothers and I have all made sure it is in the best place she can be where she has the freedom she wants and supervision that keeps me and my brothers' minds at ease.

They all know me and Atticus here, and as I walk in the door, he heads right to the ladies he knows have treats for him. After he's greeted them, we go to my mom's room.

"Jake! Did I know you were coming?" she asks as she gives me one of her warm, soft hugs that ooze love.

"Not unless you suddenly have powers to tell the future because I didn't know I was coming until about half an hour ago," I say as we go to the couch in her little living area.

Once we're sitting, she stares at me, a frown on her face, and I almost wonder if she knows what I have to say before I say it.

"Is everything okay, my boy?" She asks with so much concern that I suddenly have to spill my guts to her.

"I screwed up, Mom, and I don't know what to do."

"Well, baby, two heads are better than one. Tell me what's going on, and let's see if we can figure out a way to get you out of it."

"The problem is, I don't necessarily want to find my way out of it. What I want to do is find a way to not piss off Caden."

"Uh oh, what did you do?"

"I ran into his ex, Kassi, at Oakside, and we got to talking and catching up. That turned into me visiting her more and more every day. And before I knew it, I had real feelings for her. I tried to contact Caden, but his phone was off, and I swore I would not go any further with her without talking to him. But last night changed everything. When I tried to call him again this morning, his phone was still off."

"He's at some training because his unit is getting ready to deploy in a couple of months. Can you put everything on hold until you can talk to him? You should be able to hear from him in a week or so."

"Kassi has been through a lot since Caden, and I'm worried that if I pull back now, I'm going to lose her. She is at Oakside because she joined the army and was injured. The last thing she needs is losing a part of her support system."

That seems to get my mom's attention.

"Is that dear girl okay?" she asks, concern written all over her face.

"She's going to be fine, but backing off isn't an option. Once she's back on her feet, she will be assigned to another duty station. I'm going to follow her, Mom."

"Are you sure this isn't just some leftover teenage crush that you want to fulfill?" she asks so softly that I know she's not accusing me of anything.

"When she was dating Caden, the only feeling I had for her was like a little sister. I enjoyed hanging out with her, but that was it. I thought they were good together, but I hardly noticed her. My head sometimes still has problems reconciling that she's the same girl as back then."

Mom nods, but I can tell she's lost in thought.

"You have to talk to Caden, and no matter what, you know this is not going to go over well. Had you talked to him before something started, I don't think he would have cared. But this far down the road?" She blows out her breath.

I know she won't pick sides because she's on both of our sides. Even though she wants me to be happy and be fiercely in love, she also understands how this will affect Caden and she doesn't want him hurt either.

"Tonight, I'll try to call him again and leave him a voicemail that I need to speak to him. Hopefully, he will call because I can't wait until he gets back from deployment. Hell, if I can get Kassi to agree, by the time he comes back from deployment, we will be married."

"Jake! How are you already talking about marriage?" Mom asks.

"Because I know she's the one. I never quite understood what Granddad meant when he said by the end of the first date, Grandma was the one. But I get it now. It's one of those things that you can't get until it happens," I tell her.

"The men on my dad's side of the family always fell fast and hard," Mom says, shaking her head with a smile on her face.

We both stand, and she pulls me into her for another one of her special hugs.

"I'm very happy for you. As soon as you talk to your brother, you will have my full support." She kisses me on the cheek.

"Thanks, Mom," I say, holding her tight for a bit longer.

"Now, shoo, I have a Zumba class to get to," she says, a smile lighting up her face. She might not admit it openly, but she really does love it here.

Once I'm in my car, I sit there staring at my phone for a minute before calling Caden again. It goes to voicemail, so I leave him a voice message.

"Hey man, it's Jake. Listen, I need you to call me. I'm fine, everyone is fine, but I have something important to talk to you about and it can't wait. Hope you are doing well. Talk soon. Love you."

Hopefully, he will call as soon as he turns his phone on. The problem is I have no idea when that will be.

Killing more time before heading back to Oakside, I call my buddy Thorne. We ran a few Seal missions together and have kept in touch. He recently met his girl at a Bluebonnet festival in his buddy's hometown of all places.

"Hey, Jake," he answers, and I can tell he's got a smile on his face. I'm glad he's happy. He deserves it after everything he's been through.

Taking a moment to catch up with him before I tell him what's going on with Kassi, including the conversation I just had with my mom.

He lets out a long whistle.

"I wish I had better advice, but until you can reach your brother, you are in a bad place." He tells me what I already know.

"Yeah, I figured as much. I'd go to him if I thought it would do any good. But he's at training, according to my mom."

"So, it's just a hurry up and wait scenario," he says, chuckling. "Looks like Cupid is hitting the Seal Team guys hard this year."

Now I know the two of us aren't the only ones who have fallen in love lately.

Chapter 10

Kassi

I 'm staring out at the backyard of Oakside, completely numb. I was getting better. I was talking and was doing everything the military asked of me. But that wasn't good enough.

What was the point of it all?

When a hand rests on my shoulder, I nearly jump out of my skin. Then a moment later, Jake is kneeling on the floor in front of my chair, staring at me with a concerned look.

"Hey, I must have called your name five different times. Are you okay?" His eyes search mine for an answer that he's not going to find. At least, he's not going to find an answer that he's going to like.

Atticus comes over and rests his head on my lap, attempting to comfort me. Trembling, I hand Jake the letter that turned my world upside down. I don't think I can speak the words out loud.

Medically discharged.

Honorable discharge.

Unable to function at 100%.

My plan had always been to do my twenty years and retire. In all my imaginings, I hadn't envisioned a life after retirement, and I certainly hadn't planned that I'd be forced out so soon. I loved what I did, helping wounded soldiers make it back to their families.

"I'm so sorry," Jake whispers, handing the letter back to me.

When he stands, I think he's going to leave me alone. For a minute, I wonder if that's what I really want. But the next thing I know, he's picking me up out of the chair, cradling me in his arms, and moving us further back onto the porch to one of the wicker couches. Sitting, he puts me on his lap, wrapping his arms around me.

I know with him, I don't have to be strong because he knows what I'm going through. He got the same letter, and I'm willing to guess he had the same emotions. I'm grateful he doesn't try to tell me everything's okay. Instead, he holds me tightly to his muscular body, letting me feel my pain and sorrow and the destruction of my plans.

As I rest my head on his shoulder, the tears come suddenly drenching his shirt. Those are the tears that I didn't think I'd be able to cry. He holds me, stroking my hair, rubbing my back, and kissing the top of my head.

I'm just starting to relax and calm down, when his body goes stiff. Looking up at him, I try to figure out what's wrong. But his eyes are looking over my shoulder. Following his line of sight, that's when I see his brother Caden, my ex, staring at us with rage.

No one speaks, and it gets to a point that I can't take the silence anymore.

"Caden, what are you doing here?" I ask.

"Getting ready to deploy, so I came to see my brother. I didn't expect to find you on his lap," he says, glaring at his brother, not even bothering to look at me.

This is exactly what I was afraid of. I didn't want to get in between the two brothers, and I sure as hell am not going to be the reason to break up his family.

But I realized over the last few days letting Jake go isn't really an option anymore, either. He admitted his feelings for me, and I haven't had a chance to tell him that I feel the same way.

"Well, this isn't the place to do this. Jake, will you help me back to my room?" I ask. That seems to pull him out of whatever trance he's in, staring at his brother.

Jake stands and gently helps me to my feet, making sure I'm stable. I could get back to my room with no problem, but I think the three of us need a few minutes to concentrate on something else, so I lean on Jake more than I need to.

"Come on, Caden," I say. Once he nods, we walk with him following behind us.

While we're walking, I'm battling in my head if the brothers need to have this out or if I should step in. By the time I get to my room, I know that I'm at least going to say my piece and let the chips fall where they may.

"Jake, will you go get me some lunch? I did not make it to the dining room today," I say softly. His eyes go wide, and he stares between his brother and me, so I turn and whisper softly enough for just him to hear.

"I have a few things to say to him, too. I promise I'll be fine."

He nods, and then his face goes cold as he looks over at Caden.

"We are going to talk," Jake says to him.

"Oh, you bet we are," Caden says back to him, his tone just as chilly.

When Jake leaves, we close the door behind us, and I sit on the couch, and Caden sits on the chair beside me.

"Jake tried to call you, you know."

"Yeah, I had a voicemail. I'm heading out on deployment, so I wanted to come visit. I thought it was something to do with Mom."

"Well, I'm going to tell you my side of it," I start.

"Listen, I don't need..." He begins, but I cut him off.

"No, you *will* listen. Jake has been my rock. When he first realized that I was here, we had lunch together and caught up on everything, but why I was here. When I needed a distraction, he was there with board games. That time turned into more, and it wasn't something we planned. I need you to know there was never any feeling for him when we were together."

Caden sighs, looking down at his hands. "I do know you, and I know that there wasn't anything between you two. This just wasn't something I wanted or even expected to walk into."

"Well, maybe if you had called your brother back..." I say with a smile on my face. He just looks at me with that look he used to give me when he hated what I said, even though when he knew I was right.

"Listen, Jake is the one person in my life who understands what I'm going through. He's been in my shoes. I just got my letter today, and I really hate to admit that I need him more than ever." I hold out the letter that is still in my hand.

Caden takes one look at it, and his eyes go wide.

"Shit." He says, handing it back to me.

"I love him, Caden. Though I haven't told him. But I love him with all my heart, and I'm not letting him go without a fight. I don't care if I have to fight him or you." I say, straightening my spine, staring at him.

"You know I want my brother to be happy. He deserves it more than anyone, but for it to be you, of all people." Since there's a big smile on his face and his eyes are twinkling, I know he's teasing me.

"I still have to give him shit. And we still have to talk it out. But I'm not going to stand in your way. Just don't make family get togethers awkward," he says, standing.

Happy this conversation is over, I give him a hug. "I'll do my best at family functions."

"I'm glad you're happy and that you found your person. Now I'm going to go talk to my brother."

When he opens my door, Jake is standing right there with a tray of food in his hand. He has no idea about the conversation that we just had or any idea how it went, but his eyes lock on me. He walks in and sets the food on the coffee table for me.

"Go talk to your brother. We can talk after," I tell him.

He studies my face for a moment and then nods. Both of them disappear down the hallway, and I pray that everything will work out.

Even with Caden's blessing, I still hope with everything in me that he'll come back to me.

Chapter 11

Jake

I follow my brother out into the hallway.

"Is there somewhere we can talk?" he asks.

Knowing he's going to follow me, we go to the front door.

Lexi is at the desk, and she looks at me. While she doesn't say anything, concern is written all over her face. So, I introduce her to my brother, and then we head out to the garden.

Thankfully, no one's there, and we will have privacy.

"Why are you here?" I turn around and ask him as soon as we're past the garden gate.

"I'm getting ready to deploy, and I heard your message. At first, I thought it was something about Mom, and I wanted to see her for myself. She was my first stop. She asked if I had talked to you, and when I said no, she demanded that I come straight here to see you. I'm guessing she knows?"

"Yes, after I kept getting your voicemail, I went and talked to her because I wasn't sure what to do. Kassi needs support, and the last thing I'm going to do is step away from her when she needs me the most. There is no walking away from her, just so you know." Crossing my arms over my chest, I give him my best big brother; I'm not messing around look.

"I never should have found out the way that I did." His voice is void of all emotion.

"If you had picked up your phone or called me back, you never would have." I shoot back at him, even though I know I'm entirely to blame in this whole situation.

He shoves his hands into his pockets and starts walking down one of the paths in the garden. "Of all the people, it had to be her?"

"Well, I didn't plan it. I wasn't harboring some secret crush from all those years ago. She's a different person now, that's the person who I fell in love with. And she is who I want to marry."

His eyes snap to mine, and he studies my face before speaking again. "You're that serious about her?"

"Yes, I am. If Mom hadn't told me you were in training because you were getting ready to deploy, I would have shown up on your doorstep since you weren't answering your phone."

"Kassi's a great person. When we broke up, it was because we were going in different directions and wanted different things. There were never any ill feelings, and we stayed friends until we graduated."

"I know she told me," I tell him. My tone's softer now.

"Bottom line, I want both of you to be happy. While I never thought I'd see you with her, you deserve happiness after everything you've been through. And so does she. That said, you hurt her, and I'll kick your ass on her behalf. For the record," he says, pausing. "She didn't tell me what happened to her, and I'm not going to ask, and it's not my place. But I know it's not good if she's being medically discharged."

"She told you about that?" I ask, shocked.

"She showed me the letter."

"I found her on the back porch, completely zoned out. She just received the letter today and was in shock. When she started to cry, I couldn't take it, so I held her. That's how you found us. Right before you showed up, she had finally stopped crying."

"Yeah, I always had impeccable timing and the ability to make everything better," he says with a cocky smile, and I laugh, shaking my head.

Looking down, I see Atticus sitting on guard beside me, and he keeps looking between me and Caden. He knows Caden is family, and he knows Caden is the one to throw a ball with him when he's home. But right now, he also senses the tension.

Sighing, I take his vest off, signaling to him that he's done working for now and he can go play. He runs over to Caden and sits down, wagging his tail.

Laughing, Caden leans down and pets him, scratching behind Atticus's ears before the dog is distracted by a butterfly. Suddenly, Atticus takes off running, chasing the butterfly.

"I'm not going to stop you guys from being happy. Is it going to be weird? Yeah, probably for a while. Just bear with me. And if the path leads you guys to marriage, I would be honored to have her as part of the family."

"Not if, when. She is becoming part of the family because her saying no is not an option. If she's not ready now, I'm not going anywhere. I'll wait as long as it takes." I say it with conviction.

"Noted. I was going to see if I could stay at your place while I was here..."

"You never have to ask, and you're always welcome. You have a key. For God's sake, use it," I say, stopping short of rolling my eyes. Even though we could be fighting and arguing, I'd be even more pissed if he didn't stay with me.

"Good, because I already dropped my shit off in the guest room, and I really didn't want to repack it," he says, laughing. "It's been a long few days. I'm going to head back to the house and take a nap. You need to go get your girl because I'm pretty sure she's worried about the outcome of this."

Watching Caden walk towards the parking lot, I call Atticus over and put his vest back on. But before we leave the garden, I take a minute to stare at the front of Oakside. There's a nice breeze today, and the American flag is blowing in the wind.

In one way or another, all of us here are fighting for that flag. And all of us are fighting for the American dream, whatever that means to us.

Since I entered boot camp, I've learned over time that the dream changes. But right now, the dream I want is a wife and kids and the white picket fence. I'm ready to go in and fight for it.

Walking into Oakside, I go straight to Kassi's room. She's reading on her tablet, but I know by the way she is chewing on her lips she isn't reading and her mind is elsewhere.

I lean against the door frame and watch her for a minute, enjoying the view. When she looks up, she drops the tablet in her lap.

"Jake," she sighs as if my being here just makes everything better.

"What did you and Caden talk about?" I ask her, not trusting myself to even enter the room.

"You. Us. He wasn't mad. What did you talk about?" she asks.

"You. Us." I smile at her and step into the room.

"He wants us both happy, and he gave me his blessing," I tell her.

She smiles at me with a sparkle in her gorgeous eyes.

That smile does me in. Walking to her, I drop to my knees in front of her.

"Marry me? I don't have a ring. I didn't want to be away from you long enough to go get one, but we can pick one out together. I love you, and now, with my brother's blessing, there is nothing I want more. Marry me, and let me be your rock through all this. Whatever you want to do, I will make it happen. We can stay here or we can move anywhere. I just want to be with you." I hold her hands in mine.

"Jake, you can't be serious. We just started..."

"If you aren't ready, that's fine. Just know I'm not going anywhere, and I will ask you again and again until you are ready."

She studies my face, her brows pinched.

"You're serious?" she asks.

"When it comes to spending the rest of my life with you, I've never been more serious," I tell her.

"I love you too, and I'd love to marry you, but I'm not planning anything until I'm out of here," she says in a mock stern voice.

Jumping up, I pull her into my arms.

"I am okay with that, just as long as you agree to marry me. I can wait." Then I pull her into a passionate kiss that signals the start of our forever.

I can't wait to see what's in store for us, but I know that together, we can do anything.

Epilogue

Caden

Jake had told me about Oakside many times over the phone over the last few years. But being here in person and seeing it for myself, I actually get it.

How different could things have been for him if there had been a place like this when he needed it? But he's thriving now, and so is Kassi.

In less than a week, I have to head back to the base for my second deployment. While I'm in town, I'm supporting both of them. Today is a big day for Kassi. She's finally getting her therapy dog.

Jake's boss, Easton, met his wife here as well, and she trains the therapy dogs for most of the men and women that come out of Oakside. According to Easton, Kassi just got approval the other day, and Paisley already had a dog in mind.

Right now, Kassi is meeting Dolly. If it's a match, they will start their training together. They've been playing in the backyard of Oakside for about half an hour now and Dolly seems to be taken by Kassi. Jake has had a huge smile on his face the entire time they've been playing.

Another milestone Dolly had to pass was that she got along with Atticus. So far, that seems to be the case. Jake and Atticus both approve of Dolly, so it looks like she's here to stay.

I'm standing on the back porch out of the way but enjoying watching all the activity. I've thrown the ball around for Dolly a few times, and that seems to have made me an okay person in her book.

"It looks like Paisley has made another good match, huh?"

The most beautiful girl I've ever seen steps up beside me on the porch. She's young, possibly way too young for me. Is she even eighteen? Fuck, but is she gorgeous.

"Yeah, it seems so," I say. How do you know them? Do you have someone here you're visiting?"

She giggles, and it's such a sweet sound.

"I visit everyone. While I attend college in Savannah, I volunteer at Oakside. It's one of the rules for me to stay with my brother while I'm in school. Not that I can complain. I love being able to help out here."

"What are you going to school for?" I ask, wanting to keep her talking.

"Photography and Business. I'm in my fourth year."

"So, do you want to photograph weddings and stuff?" I'm curious, plus I want to study her face some more.

"There's money in wedding photography, but I don't just want to photograph people. I've been photographing food for the last few years for an online publication. And I really love landscape photography. Animals are fun, too. But people, not so much."

I laugh at the cute way she crinkles her nose when she says people. But what really captures my attention is how her eyes light up when she talks about photographing landscapes. It's obvious where her true passion lies.

"You should go with what makes you happy. Life's too short to be stuck in a miserable career," I give her my honest opinion.

"That's what my brother says. He's been really supportive."

"What's your name?" I want to know more about her.

"It's Lucy. What's your name?"

"Caden."

While I'm here visiting, we spend hours together over the next week. Pretty much any spare time I have, Lucy and I are together, talking and getting to know each other.

Even though I really like her and am seriously attracted to her, I've had to fight every instinct in me not to kiss her. More than anything, I would love to take her on a date. But I'm not going to be that asshole to lead her on and then leave for deployment.

Every day, we end up on the back porch, sitting and talking as we watch Jake and Kassi training with Dolly.

"Were you ever going to ask me out to dinner or try to kiss me?" Lucy asks me boldly out of nowhere, and my jaw drops.

When I recover, I offer her the truth.

"I like you. If I wasn't deploying, I'd ask you out in a heartbeat. But I am going, and I can't do that to you. Getting your hopes up and then leaving is a dick move."

She bites her bottom lip as she stares out over the lawn for a few minutes.

How can her biting that plump, kissable bottom lip drive me crazy?

"What if I want to write to you while you're gone and get to know you more? Then, when you get back, we can see where we're at."

"I'd like that. Can you give me your address? I won't have mine until I get there, but I can write to you as soon as I have it. Give me your phone number and email, too. I might be able to call and e-mail you, though that might be limited."

She pulls a notebook from her purse and writes it all down before handing me a piece of paper.

I look down at the paper she just handed me.

Lucy Carr.

No. What are the fucking odds?

"There you are, Lucy. Brooke told me I might find you out here."

I know that voice before I even look up.

"Noah?" I ask.

"Caden?" He says, shocked. "What are you doing here?" He walks over and gives me a manly hug.

"Visiting my brother before I head out on another deployment." I point to Jake out on the front lawn.

"Oh shit, you're Jake's brother? In all this time, I never put it together." He looks at me, a little dazed.

"What are you doing here?" I ask him, noting he's got some scars on his arm and up his neck. But hell, I don't think any of us walk away from the military without some new scars.

"My wife and I run the place," he says, smiling.

Then, it all clicks into place. Noah is Lucy's older brother, the one she's staying with.

"How do you two know each other?" Lucy asks me like my world's not spinning out of control.

Taking a seat, I'm at a loss for what to tell her.

Thankfully, Noah takes over.

"We went to boot camp together and ended up being stationed together. He had my back through my first deployment. Before my last one, we ended up at separate duty stations. But after my accident, I lost touch with a lot of people, him included," Noah says with a hint of regret in his voice.

"Hey, before I forget, Lexi was looking for you. She needs your help with something. She's in her office." Noah tells Lucy.

Standing, she looks at me one last time before disappearing inside. Noah and I spend some time catching up and he gives me his address and tells me to write and to keep in touch this time.

As I'm leaving, I get stopped by Lucy. She hands me an envelope.

"I don't care that you and my brother know each other. I'm still going to write to you. You better send me your address. Don't think for one minute that I don't have ways of getting it. So let me know it when you do!" She says it with determination and grit before she walks away.

I'm fucked if I do and fucked up if I don't.

I know Noah will have me by the balls if he finds out how I feel about his little sister. On the other hand, Lucy already has me by the heart.

Fuck.

***

Get more Jake and Kassi. **Grab their Bonus Story now!** - https://www.kacirose.com/Jake-Bonus

Ready for Caden's story? **Grab it in Saving Caden.**

Want Thorne's story? Get it in Defending Destiny by Eve London: https://geni.us/DefendingDestiny

***

This book was originally published as Saving Kassi in the Seal Team Alpha Series.

Eight of your favorite authors have teamed up to bring you a steamy, Navy SEAL filled romance series! Grab this series and get ready to fall in love with the sexy men of SEAL Team Alpha!

Protecting Lila by Shaw Hart - https://geni.us/ProtectingLila

Claiming Jane by Hope Ford - http://mybook.to/ClaimingJane

Defending Destiny by Eve London: https://geni.us/DefendingDestiny

Guarding Gemma by Fern Fraser: https://geni.us/GuardingGemma

Keeping   Kelsie   by   Kat   Baxter: https://books2read.com/u/mBA95v

Saving Selyne by Kameron Claire: https://geni.us/SecuringSelyne

Rescuing   Roxy   by   Cameron Hart: https://books2read.com/u/3nGaoe

Connect with Kaci Rose

Website

Kaci Rose's Book Shop

Facebook

Kaci Rose Reader's Facebook Group

TikTok

Instagram

Goodreads

Book Bub

Join Kaci Rose's VIP List (Newsletter)

About Kaci Rose

    Kaci Rose writes steamy contemporary romances mostly set in small towns. She grew up in Florida but now lives in a cabin in the mountains of East Tennessee.

She is a mom to five kids, a rescue dog who is scared of his own shadow, an energetic young German Shepherd who is still in training, a sleepy old hound who adopted her, and a reluctant indoor cat. Kaci loves to travel, and her goal is to visit all 50 states before she turns 50. She has 17 more to go, mostly in the Midwest and on the West Coast!

She also writes steamy cowboy romances as Kaci M. Rose.

Other Books by Kaci Rose

See all of Kaci Rose's Books

Mountain Men of Whiskey River
Take Me To The River – Axel and Emelie
Take Me To The Cabin – Pheonix and Jenna
Take Me To The Lake – Cash and Hope
Taken by The Mountain Man - Cole and Jana
Take Me To The Mountain – Bennett and Willow
Take Me To The Cliff – Jack and Sage
Take Me To The Edge – Storm and River
Take Me To The Valley

Oakside Military Heroes Series
Saving Noah – Lexi and Noah

Saving Easton – Easton and Paisley
Saving Teddy – Teddy and Mia
Saving Levi – Levi and Mandy
Saving Gavin – Gavin and Lauren
Saving Logan – Logan and Faith
Saving Zane

Oakside Shorts
Saving Mason - Mason and Paige
Saving Ethan – Bri and Ethan
Saving Jake – Jake and Kassi
Saving Caden

Club Red – Short Stories
Daddy's Dare – Knox and Summer
Sold to my Ex's Dad - Evan and Jana
Jingling His Bells – Zion and Emma
Watching You – Ella and Brooks, Connor, and Finn

Club Red: Chicago
Elusive Dom - Carter and Gemma
Forbidden Dom – Gage and Sky

Mountain Men of Mustang Mountain
(Series Written with Dylann Crush and Eve London)
February is for Ford – Ford and Luna
April is For Asher – Asher and Jenna
June is for Jensen – Jensen and Courtney

August is for Ace – Ace and Everly
October is for Owen – Owen and Kennedy
December is for Dean – Dean and Holly

Mustang Mountain Riders
(Series Written with Eve London)
February's Ride With Bear – Bear and Emerson
April's Ride With Stone
enotS-June's Ride With LightningAugust's Ride With Arrow
October's Ride With Atlas
December's Ride With Scar

Chasing the Sun Duet
Sunrise – Kade and Lin
Sunset – Jasper and Brynn

Rock Stars of Nashville
She's Still The One – Dallas and Austin

Accidental Series
Accidental Sugar Daddy – Owen and Ellie
The Billionaire's Accidental Nanny - Mari and Dalton

The Italian Mafia Princesses
Midnight Rose - Ruby and Orlando

Standalone Books
Texting Titan - Denver and Avery
Stay With Me Now – David and Ivy
Committed Cowboy – Whiskey Run Cowboys

Stalking His Obsession - Dakota and Grant
Falling in Love on Route 66 - Weston and Rory

Please Leave a Review!

I love to hear from my readers! Please **head over to your favorite store and leave a review** of what you thought of this book! Reviews also appreciated on BookBub and Goodreads!

Made in the USA
Columbia, SC
23 September 2024

42084013R00052